Rattle and Hum
Robot Detectives

Frank Rodgers

Collins

... for more ... from Collins

Jessy Runs Away • *Best Friends* • **Rachel Anderson**
Ivana the Inventor • *Ernest the Heroic Lion Tamer* • **Damon Burnard**
Two Hoots • *Almost Goodbye Guzzler* • **Helen Cresswell**
Shadows on the Barn • **Sara Garland**
Nora Bone • *The Mystery of Lydia Dustbin's Diamonds* • **Brough Girling**
Thing on Two Legs • *Thing in a Box* • **Diana Hendry**
Desperate for a Dog • *More Dog Trouble* • **Rose Impey**
Georgie and the Dragon • *Georgie and the Planet Raider* • **Julia Jarman**
Cowardy Cowardy Cutlass • *Free With Every Pack* • **Robin Kingsland**
Mossop's Last Chance • *Mum's the Word* • **Michael Morpurgo**
Hiccup Harry • *Harry Moves House* • **Chris Powling**
Rattle and Hum in Double Trouble • **Frank Rodgers**
Our Toilet's Haunted • **John Talbot**
Rhyming Russell • *Messages* • **Pat Thomson**
Monty the Dog Who Wears Glasses • *Monty's Ups and Downs* • **Colin West**
Ging Gang Goolie, it's an Alien • *Stone the Crows, it's a Vacuum Cleaner* • **Bob Wilson**

First published by A & C Black Ltd in 1996
Published by Collins in 1996
10 9 8 7 6 5 4 3
Collins is an imprint of HarperCollins*Publishers* Ltd,
77–85 Fulham Palace Road, Hammersmith, London W6 8JB

ISBN 0 00 675171-7

A CIP record for this title is available from the British Library.
Printed and bound in Great Britain by
Caledonian International Book Manufacturing Ltd, Glasgow

Chapter One

It all began in the rowdy racket of the robot factory one Friday afternoon.

Two rather rickety robots rolled past Ernest Pimm, the checker.

Ernest was daydreaming about working somewhere quieter – like a disco – so he didn't notice.

But Mr Gumboyle, the mean and nasty sharp-eared director, did.

The whole factory came to a standstill and Ernest woke up.

'You've been snoozing on the job, Pimm!' shouted Mr Gumboyle.

'You did!' roared Mr Gumboyle.
'Listen to them!'

One robot sounded like tin cans tied to a wedding car and the other robot sounded like an electric toothbrush.

'Are you arguing with me, Pimm?' snarled Mr Gumboyle.

'Er . . . no,' squeaked Ernest.

After that, Ernest was a nervous wreck.

He shook so much that his glasses bounced up and down on his nose as if they were on a trampoline.

This meant that he couldn't see very well.

As he was typing out the labels for the defective robots, he missed the letter F and hit T in its place.

Instead of labels that said 'defective', he stuck on labels which looked much the same but actually meant something completely and utterly different.

Then, instead of sending them packing, back to the Assembly Department to be dismantled, he sent them to the PACKING DEPARTMENT.

Mr Box, the packer, took one look at the two robots and smiled.

He packed the rickety robots into a crate and stuck a nice big label on the front.

Chapter Two

Down at the Police Station, Sergeant Salt was feeling very pleased with himself.

Only that morning his police squad had caught three baddies red-handed.

Percy Pussyfoot, the cat burglar, had been apprehended by Constable Copper.

Cash O'Fake, the counterfeiter, had been arrested by Detective Bobby.

And Nick Gamp, the umbrella thief, had been nabbed by Detective Peeler.

Sergeant Salt had been so pleased that he had given his squad a week's holiday.

'It'll be nice and quiet with those three crooks behind bars,' he thought. But he was wrong.

Just as the sergeant was having a cup of tea and a biscuit there was a loud

The door flew open and a large crate was pushed inside by a puffing and panting postman.

'Special delivery!' he croaked, and crept out again, crimson-faced.

Before the sergeant could say anything, the top of the crate burst open. Up popped the robots.

'Who are you?' demanded the sergeant.

The robots looked at each other then back at the sergeant.

'Rattle and Hum?' said the sergeant faintly. 'And . . . er . . . what are you doing here?'

The robots clambered out of the crate and pointed proudly at their labels.

Sergeant Salt nearly choked. 'Detectives?' he spluttered, spitting his biscuit into his tea.

But before he could say anything else, there was another loud

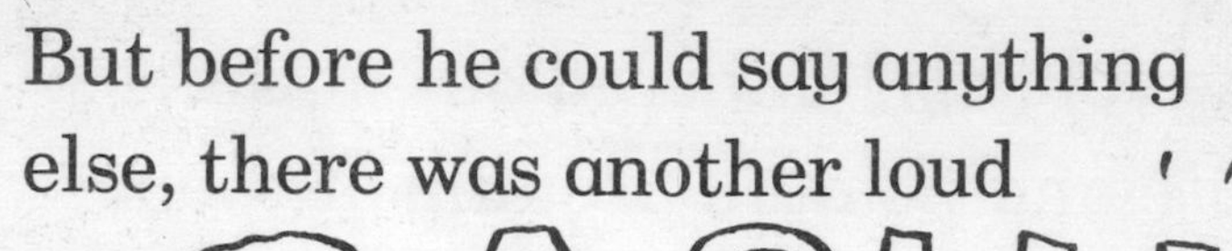

The door flew open again and in stormed Cannonball Kate, the cook from *The Treasure Island Cafe* across the street.

Sergeant Salt grabbed the phone.

Sergeant Salt was too embarrassed to tell Kate that all his squad were on holiday, so in desperation he asked Rattle and Hum to take charge of the case.

Chapter Three

The two robots clanked across the road to the cafe with Kate.
'What's been stolen?'
they asked.

'Me cutlass . . .

. . . and me spare set of false teeth, of course,' yelled Kate.

‘I use me
cutlass for
a-choppin’
the meat . . .

. . . and the
false teeth
for a-cuttin’ out
nice biscuit shapes.’

‘I left them here last night and this
morning they were gone!’

Kate sat down at the kitchen table and a tear trickled down her nose.

'Oh dear, I've had such a sad life,' sniffled Kate. 'You see, my sister and I were orphans who ran away from a children's home.'

'Unfortunately, we ran in opposite directions . . .

. . . and I haven't seen her since.'

'But who would want to steal a cutlass and a set of false teeth?' wailed Kate.

'A toothless pirate?' suggested Rattle.

'Do you know any?' asked Hum.

'Well . . . there's Peg-leg Pascoe,' said Kate. 'But he got a set of wooden teeth to match his leg so it can't be him.

And there's Cap'n George Gumsy.

But it won't be him either . . . he took a set of teeth from a shark. Calls himself Cap'n Jaws Gumsy now. They are the only toothless pirates around,' said Kate.

Just then they heard a scratching noise coming from the bread-bin. Rattle looked inside.

'Is the toad that's swimming in the soup trespassing too?' asked Hum.

'What!' cried Kate. 'Where did that come from?'

Rattle began to rattle loudly. 'What are you doing?' asked Hum.

'Thinking hard,' replied Rattle. 'Trying to solve this problem.'

'You'll shake yourself to bits!' said Hum.

'You've got a screw loose,' said Hum as she fixed it back on.

'Aha!' said Rattle, 'and now that my bottom's been fixed . . . the mystery rattle has gone! Brilliant!'

Chapter Four

Back at the Police Station, Sergeant Salt was happily munching another biscuit and drinking a fresh cup of tea when the door flew open again.

'Who?' asked the sergeant, so startled that he dropped his biscuit right into his tea.

'Those two faulty robots!' yelled Mr Gumboyle. 'They were sent here!'

'F-f-faulty?' stammered the sergeant.

'Yes, faulty!' roared Mr Gumboyle.

'Defective?' gulped the sergeant. 'B-b-but they said they were *detectives*.'

'That's Pimm the checker's fault,' snarled Mr Gumboyle. 'He put on the wrong labels!'

'Oh dear,' said the sergeant. 'I've just given them a case to solve.'

'What?' roared Mr Gumboyle. 'If anyone hears about this I'll be a laughing stock. Where did they go?'

'To *The Treasure Island Cafe* across the street,' replied the sergeant.

'You'd better hope I find them,' spat out Mr Gumboyle. 'Because if I don't, I'll have you fired from the force!'

'Fired from the force? Oo-er! What a nasty thought,' gulped the sergeant.

Chapter Five

Back at the cafe,
Hum was humming
loudly. 'I've been
thinking,' she said.

'Be careful,' warned
Rattle. 'Remember
what happened to me.'

'What?' asked Hum.

'Whoops!' said Hum. 'I feel a draught!'

Rattle fixed it back on and Hum
stopped humming.

'That's better!' she cried. 'Now I can hear myself think. Right, where was I? Oh yes . . . I was thinking there might be a connection between the disappearance of your choppers and the appearance of these animals. Do you recognise them, Kate?'

Kate shook her head. 'They don't look familiar to me,' she said.

She tapped out the word 'familiar' on Rattle's chest-keyboard.

ZZZ . . . out came a piece of paper. It was an extract from a dictionary.

'I've got it! These animals are a witch's familiars!' cried Rattle. 'Brilliant!' He clapped Hum on the back so hard her bottom nearly fell off again.

'You mean there's been a witch in my kitchen?' cried Kate. 'A-rummagin' through my recipes and a-tiptoein' among my tea cups?'

'We don't know, but we're going to find out,' said Rattle and Hum. They scooped up the animals and hurried out of the back door, just as Mr Gumboyle came in by the front.

Chapter Six

Back at the Police Station, Sergeant Salt had just made himself another cup of tea when Rattle and Hum arrived back from the cafe. 'You two aren't detectives!' he yelled, taking a big bite of biscuit in annoyance.

'Yes we are,' replied Rattle. 'We've already begun to solve Kate's mysterious robbery. We've got clues!'

'Yes,' said Hum. 'There's a witch involved. We found these animals in Kate's kitchen. They are a witch's familiars.'

'Can you tell us if there are any witches in town, Sergeant?'

'As far as I know, there are only two witches in town. Arabella Bottomless-Pitt and Belladonna Broomstick.'

'Here are their addresses,' said the sergeant. 'Good luck – you'll need it.'

'Thank you, Sergeant,' said Rattle and Hum. 'Don't worry, we'll have this case cracked before you can say *Jack Robotson*.'

Moments later Mr Gumboyle came crashing through the door.

'You just missed them,' said the sergeant, smiling. 'They've gone to see a couple of witches.'

'What?' cried Mr Gumboyle. 'I'll have you sacked for this, mark my words!' He snatched the witches' addresses and galloped out of the door.

Chapter Seven

Meanwhile, Rattle and Hum had just arrived at Arabella Bottomless-Pitt's house. Arabella was a very friendly witch and she invited the robots into her kitchen.

Hum showed Arabella the cat and the toad. 'Are these your familiars by any chance?' she asked.

'No, dearie,' replied Arabella. 'I've got mine right here.' And from her pocket she produced . . .

. . . a rattlesnake . . .

. . . and a tarantula.

'Want to kiss them?' she asked.

'Er, no thanks,' said Rattle and Hum. 'We really have to be going.'

The two robots hurried on to Belladonna Broomstick's house. But they soon discovered that the second witch wasn't as nice as the first.

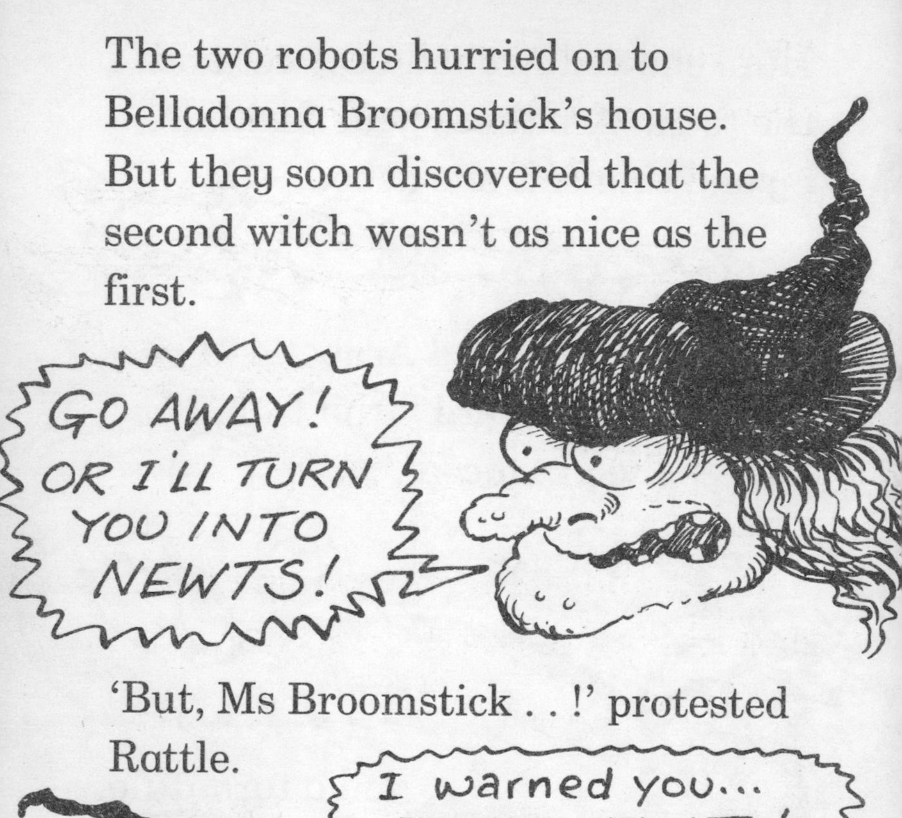

'But, Ms Broomstick . . !' protested Rattle.

The robots vanished in a puff of green smoke and in their place stood two metal newts.

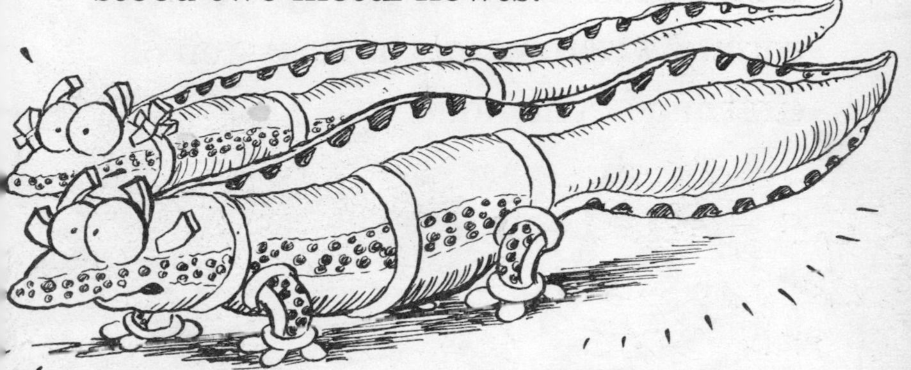

The cat and the toad took one look and ran out of the door, totally confused.

'Wait for us!' squeaked Rattle and Hum.

Round the corner and up another street they ran on their short metal legs. At last they caught up with the cat and the toad on the doorstep of a strange little house.

The sign on the door said:

Bubbly Cauldron

New Witch on the block.

'Oh no!' squeaked Hum. 'Not another one!'

Before they could escape, the door flew open and there stood Bubbly Cauldron.
'Oh!' she gasped, 'my little darlings!'
She scooped up the cat and the toad. 'You've come back,' she said.

Then she noticed the newts.

'Aha! This looks like Belladonna's handiwork,' she said.

Rattle and Hum nodded miserably.

'No problem,' cried Bubbly and she tried a spell.

'Whoops,' she said, 'let's try that again, shall we?'

'Er . . . one more time for luck?'

'I'll get the hang of spelling one of these days,' laughed Bubbly. 'Anyway, thank you so much for returning my familiars. Do come inside and have a cup of Bubbly's brew. It'll put a spring in your sprockets!'

Rattle and Hum stepped inside and Bubbly closed the door.

None of them saw Mr Gumboyle storm past on his way to Belladonna's house.

Chapter Eight

'Tell me, Ms Cauldron,' asked Rattle, 'when your pets vanished did anything else appear in their place?'

Rattle and Hum grinned at one another and explained.

'You see,' said Hum, 'when your spell went wrong, your familiars flew to Cannonball Kate's kitchen.'

'And her choppers flew here,' said Rattle.

'Amazing!' cried Bubbly, then a tear trickled down her face.

'I've had a sad life,' sniffed Bubbly. 'Nothing's gone right since I ran away from a children's home and lost my sister.'

'Lost your sister!' chorused the robots. 'Hooray!'

'Hoo-blooming-ray?' cried Bubbly, aghast. 'It's no cheering matter, you two!'

The robots took Bubbly by the arm and in their best police tones said, 'Would you care to accompany us to the Police Station, madam?'

Chapter Nine

No sooner had they arrived back at the Police Station when Cannonball Kate rushed in again.

'Oh!' she exclaimed in delight. 'You've found me chopper and me choppers. Wonderful! Thanks a million! I'm such a pleased pirate!'

Then she noticed Bubbly.

'Oh . . . can it be . . ?'
she gasped.
'Yes . . . it is!'

'Beauticia!' cried Bubbly, and the two sisters hugged for joy and danced a witchy waltz and a piratical polka in delight.

Sergeant Salt was delighted too. 'Brilliant work,' he said.

But before they could finish, the door opened and in scampered a rather nasty-looking newt.

The sergeant recognised it at once. 'Gumboyle!' he gasped.

The newt pointed at Rattle and Hum. 'You two are going to be dismantled!' it squeaked furiously.

'But we're not faulty any more,' protested the robots. Unfortunately, Mr Gumboyle had made them so nervous that they began to shake and . . .

RATTLE and HUM again.

Bubbly Cauldron picked up the newt.

'In fact,' she went on, 'I've a good mind to turn you into a wriggly little titchy squidgy worm . . .

. . . or an itsy-bitsy, bug-eyed beetle . . .

. . . or perhaps even a wart on the end of someone's nose! How would you like that?'

'No, no!' squeaked the newt. 'Don't! I'll be good . . . really I will! I won't boss Ernest Pimm about any more and Rattle and Hum can stay here as long as they like! Honest!'

'Hooray!' cheered the robots, and they danced round the room rattling and humming like mad, but holding on to their bottoms, just in case.

'Very well, then,' said Bubbly and she waved her hands in the air.

Bubbly tried again, and this time it worked.

'Oh, thank you, thank you,' stammered Mr Gumboyle. 'I'm back to normal! A changed man! I just feel so . . . NICE!'

'How would you two ladies like to come back to the robot factory with me?' he said brightly. 'We could have tea with my checker chum Ernest Pimm.'

'That would be scrumdiddly!' chorused the sisters. They thanked Rattle and Hum once again and hurried off to the factory.

When they had gone Sergeant Salt turned to Rattle and Hum. 'Welcome to the police force,' he said.

'Of course you aren't,' grinned the sergeant. 'You're ROBOT DETECTIVES.'

Rattle and Hum were so thrilled that their tin chests swelled and they rattled and hummed so much that . . .

. . . their bottoms fell off with pride.

'Time for a cup of tea and a biscuit,' said the sergeant.